Simple Machines to the Rescue

Wheels and Axles to the Rescue

by Sharon Thales

Consultant:
Louis A. Bloomfield, PhD
Professor of Physics
University of Virginia
Charlottesville, Virginia

Capstone
press®

Mankato, Minnesota

First Facts is published by Capstone Press,
151 Good Counsel Drive, P.O. Box 669, Mankato, Minnesota 56002.
www.capstonepress.com

Library of Congress Cataloging-in-Publication Data
Thales, Sharon.
   Wheels and axles to the rescue / Sharon Thales.
   p. cm.—(First facts. Simple machines to the rescue)
   Includes bibliographical references and index.
   ISBN-13: 978-0-7368-6751-1 (hardcover)
   ISBN-10: 0-7368-6751-1 (hardcover)
   1. Wheels—Juvenile literature. 2. Axles—Juvenile literature. I. Title. II. Series.
TJ181.5.T47 2007
621.8—dc22
                                         2006021504

Summary: Describes wheels and axles, including what they are, how they work, past uses, and
   common uses of these simple machines today.

Editorial Credits
Becky Viaene, editor; Thomas Emery, designer; Patrick D. Dentinger, illustrator; Jo Miller,
   photo researcher/photo editor

Photo Credits
Capstone Press/Karon Dubke, 5, 6, 12, 18–19, 21 (all); TJ Thoraldson Digital Photography, cover
Corbis/epa/Waltraud Grubitzsch, 20; Joseph Sohm/ChromoSohm Inc., 15
Index Stock Imagery/Arni Katz, 10
Ron Kimball Stock/Ron Kimball, 13
Shutterstock/Jaimie Duplass, 17

1 2 3 4 5 6 12 11 10 09 08 07

Table of Contents

A Helpful Wheel and Axle 4

Work It 7

A Wheel and Axle in Time 8

What Would We Do Without Wheels and Axles? 12

Working Together 16

Wheels and Axles Everywhere 19

Amazing but True! 20

Hands On: Working with a Wheel and Axle 21

Glossary 22

Read More 23

Internet Sites 23

Index 24

A Helpful Wheel and Axle

You're helping your mom make pizza. The dough is in a big ball. How can you flatten it?

Wheel and axle to the rescue!

Use a rolling pin. The **wheel** and **axle** in the rolling pin help you spread out the dough.

Work It

A wheel and an axle make a **simple machine**. Simple machines have one or no moving parts. Machines are used to make **work** easier.

Work is using a **force** to move an object. Together, wheels and axles do work by moving objects.

Wheel and Axle Fact

Not sure what wheels and axles look like? A wheel is a round disc. An axle is a long bar that attaches to the center of a wheel.

A Wheel and Axle in Time

Thousands of years ago, Egyptians wanted a faster way to make clay pots.

Wheel and axle to the rescue!

Egyptians placed wheels on top of axles. Then they put lumps of clay in the middle of the wheels. Next, they turned the wheels while quickly shaping the clay into pots.

Wheel and Axle

Wheel and Axle

Hundreds of years ago, grinding grain into flour by hand was a hard job. Wheels and axles came to the rescue.

People made large wooden axles and water wheels that rested in streams. The streams turned the wheels and axles. The axles helped turn huge stones inside the buildings that crushed grain into flour.

What Would We Do Without Wheels and Axles?

Wheels and axles help you travel short distances quickly. You couldn't use your bike or inline skates without wheels and axles.

Wheels and axles also help people travel long distances. Trucks, cars, buses, and airplanes move with the help of wheels and axles.

Ready for a ride? Some wheels and axles are built for fun. Many rides at the fair, like the ferris wheel, use wheels and axles.

Wheel and Axle Fact

Not all wheels and axles look the same. The blades on top of a helicopter aren't round. But they are part of a wheel that spins quickly around an axle. Helicopters come to the rescue to help injured and sick people get to hospitals quickly.

Working Together

The grass in your yard is getting too long. Your parents need a **complex machine,** called a mower, to cut it.

Your dad pushes the lever down. He pulls on a cord connected to a pulley to start the mower. Wheels and axles help the mower move. A sharp wedge under the mower cuts the grass.

Wheel and Axle Buddies

Six kinds of simple machines combine to make almost every machine there is.

- **Inclined plane**–a slanting surface that is used to move objects to different levels

- **Lever**–a bar that turns on a resting point and is used to lift items

- **Pulley**–a grooved wheel turned by a rope, belt, or chain that often moves heavy objects

- **Screw**–an inclined plane wrapped around a post that usually holds objects together

- **Wedge**–an inclined plane that moves to split things apart or push them together

- **Wheel and axle**–a wheel that turns around a bar to move objects

Lever

Wheel and Axle

Wheels and Axles Everywhere

Wheels and axles are easy to see on some machines, such as bikes. But wheels and axles can also be hidden.

Pencil sharpeners, doorknobs, and combination locks have wheels and axles. Wheels and axles help you every day.

When a pet's legs don't work properly, wheels and axles can help them get around. Dog wheelchairs come in sizes to fit big and little dogs. People can buy wheelchairs for their cats, rabbits, and other pets too.

Hands On: Working with a Wheel and Axle

What You Need

8-inch (20-centimeter) square of light cardboard, sharp pencil, scissors

What You Do

1. Draw the biggest circle you can on the cardboard.
2. Cut out the circle. This is your wheel.
3. Carefully poke the pencil through the center of the circle. Now you have a wheel and axle.
4. Hold the pencil with the edge of the circle resting on a table. When you turn one end of the pencil, the circle should rotate too.

The pencil is an axle and the cardboard circle is a wheel. When you turn the pencil, it turns the circle. The circle is larger around than the pencil, so the circle moves farther across the table than the pencil alone.

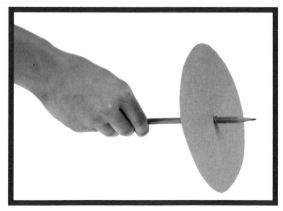

Glossary

axle (AK-suhl)—a bar in the center of a wheel around which the wheel turns

complex machine (KOM-pleks muh-SHEEN)—a machine made of two or more simple machines

force (FORSS)—a push or a pull

simple machine (SIM-puhl muh-SHEEN)—a tool with one or no moving parts that moves an object when you push or pull; wheels and axles are simple machines.

wheel (WEEL)—a round disc; a wheel turns around an axle and moves a greater distance than the axle.

work (WURK)—when a force moves an object

Read More

Dahl, Michael. *Tires, Spokes, and Sprockets: A Book about Wheels and Axles.* Amazing Science. Minneapolis: Picture Window Books, 2006.

Oxlade, Chris. *Wheels.* Useful Machines. Chicago: Heinemann Library, 2003.

Tieck, Sarah. *Wheels and Axles.* Simple Machines. Edina, Minn.: Abdo, 2006.

Internet Sites

FactHound offers a safe, fun way to find Internet sites related to this book. All of the sites on FactHound have been researched by our staff.

Here's how:

1. Visit *www.facthound.com*

2. Choose your grade level.

3. Type in this book ID **0736867511** for age-appropriate sites. You may also browse subjects by clicking on letters, or by clicking on pictures and words.

4. Click on the **Fetch It** button.

FactHound will fetch the best sites for you!

Index

appearance, 7

bikes, 12, 19

clay pots, 8
combination locks, 19
complex machines, 16

doorknobs, 19

Egyptians, 8

force, 7

grain, 11

helicopters, 14
historical uses, 8, 11

inline skates, 12

levers, 16, 17

modern uses, 4, 12, 13, 14, 16, 19, 20
mowers, 16

pencil sharpeners, 19
pet wheelchairs, 20
pottery wheels, 8
pulleys, 16, 17

rides, 14
rolling pins, 4

simple machines, 7, 17

traveling, 12, 13, 14

water wheels, 11
wedges, 16, 17
work, 7